Jou

PABLO

WRITTEN BY REBEKAH ANDERSON

The Journey Series

As I began writing this series, the word "journey" resonated deeply with me for several reasons. Journey signifies traveling from one place to another, and I envision this series transporting readers into the lives of people worldwide.

Millions globally grow up without hearing the Gospel. Through these books, I aim to provide a glimpse into diverse cultures and lives transformed by God's redemption. May these stories inspire greater involvement in global missions.

The word "journey" also reminds me of our spiritual path.

God lovingly guides us as we mature in faith, becoming who He intends us to be. The Lord remains constant across cultures, languages, and nations. I hope this series highlights God's transformative power, illuminating lives once shrouded in darkness with the Gospel's light.

My prayer is that these fictitious stories inspire you to allow God to use you in the lives of those around you and worldwide. The Gospel is meant to be shared.

- Rebekah Anderson

Dedication

The word "journey" holds a profound significance for me due to my baby niece, Journey, who bore this name. I dedicate this series to her memory. Though her life was fleeting, God has used Journey's brief existence to encourage and challenge us all.

Her parents' unwavering faith has exemplified the strength found in God's presence, even in the darkest of trials.

Our never-failing God, sovereignly uses all things – including the most painful – to bring glory to Himself. May this series inspire the people of God to rally behind the millions in dire need of the transformative power of the Gospel message.

Acknowledgements

I extend my heartfelt gratitude to my parents, Gary and Deanna Ellison, who raised me in a Christ-centered home. As a pastor and missionary, my father's dedication to God's work profoundly impacted my life. Growing up surrounded by godly influences shaped my perspective on eternity.

I'm deeply thankful that my parents obeyed God's call, allowing me to experience ministry in a positive light. My mother deserves special recognition for nurturing my love for reading and writing. Her tireless efforts in homeschooling my seven siblings and me, from grade school through graduation, are a testament to her unwavering faith and tenacity.

My parents provided us with an abundance of engaging reading materials, fostering a love for adventure and learning. Their influence has been invaluable.

I also express sincere appreciation to my husband, Jonathan Anderson, whose vision for this series inspired me to craft stories that offer a glimpse into the lives of people in countries without Christ. His obedience to God's call on his life has both encouraged and challenged me.

Lastly, I thank Joy Wahl, a dear friend and diligent editor, who generously devoted her time to refining this book. Her insights, gained from sharing experiences with us in Mexico, enriched my writing.

Contents

PREFACE

In the vibrant city of Guadalajara, Mexico, where colorful markets burst with life and ancient traditions weave through the streets, a young boy named Pablo felt a profound sense of loss and isolation. His once-bright eyes, which had gleamed with boundless curiosity, were now clouded by the weight of despair. The struggles his family faced to make ends meet, coupled with his mounting doubts and fears, had cast a shadow over his young heart.

As Pablo meandered through Guadalajara's winding streets, a divine encounter awaited him, one that would change his life's trajectory. Amidst the city's rich cultural tapestry, where the air was filled with the aroma of mole and fresh tortillas, and joyous sounds of laughter and music filled the streets, hope began to emerge. A chance meeting with a stranger, guided by God's hand, would soon reveal the profound and unrelenting love of a Heavenly Father, setting in motion events that would forever alter Pablo's path.

Join us on Pablo's transformative journey as we step into the lives of those who inhabit a world vastly different from our own. Through his story, gain insight into the heart of Guadalajara – a city pulsing with tradition and resilience – and witness how his despair is rewritten into a powerful testament of hope and divine love. This book serves as a bridge, connecting readers with Guadalajara's culture and community, sharing universal threads of faith, hope, and redemption.

"Therefore if any man be in Christ, he is a new creature: old things are passed away; behold, all things are become new."

2 Corinthians 5:17

Chapter One

Day of the Dead

Pablo crept into the living room, his eyes adjusting to the soft glow of candles and twinkling lights. He was almost eight years old and was beginning to understand the traditions of Day of the Dead, especially now that his mother had her own offering. The air was thick with the scent of marigolds and incense. Before him, the altar seemed to shimmer, a vibrant tapestry of memories and love.

His mother's favorite things were arranged with tender care: her worn blue apron, a brightly colored scarf, and a photograph of her kind smile. Pablo's heart ached as he gazed upon the familiar objects, each one a bittersweet reminder of her presence. It had almost been one year since his mother had passed away, but it seemed like she had just left him.

His grandmother had outdone herself this year, crafting an offering that seemed to capture the essence of his mother's spirit. The colorful crepe paper banners, the delicate sugar skulls, and the steaming plates of her favorite foods all blended together in a bittersweet tribute.

Pablo's eyes wandered to the photograph of his mother, her dark hair pulled back, her brown eyes sparkling with warmth. He remembered the way she would smile at him, the way her hands would cradle his face. A lump formed in his throat as he whispered, "Mamá... I miss you." He lifted his hand to his face to wipe away a stubborn tear.

He felt a gentle touch on his shoulder, and looked up to see his grandmother beside him, her eyes shining with tears. "She's still with us, Pablo," she whispered, "In our hearts, and our memories. We honor her today, and every day." He could still smell garlic and chili peppers on his grandmother's wrinkled hands. She had been working all day to prepare this special meal.

Pablo nodded, tears blurring his vision. He felt the weight of his grief, but also the comfort of his family's love. Together, they would navigate this first Day of the Dead without his mother.

Pablo looked up at his grandmother with curiosity in his eyes. "Why do we light the candles, Abuela?" he asked softly. He had heard this answer before, but he wanted to hear it again.

His grandmother's expression softened as she replied, "We light the candles, hijo, to guide the spirits back home. You see, on

Day of the Dead, the veil between the worlds is thin. Our loved ones can return to visit us, and the candles help them find their way."

Pablo's eyes widened, fascinated. "Like a path of light?"

She nodded, smiling. "Exactly, hijo. The candles illuminate the path, so our loved ones can navigate the darkness and join us once more. We believe their spirits return to share in our feasting, to enjoy the foods and drinks they loved in life."

Pablo's gaze returned to the altar, where his mother's photograph smiled back at him. He felt a sense of comfort, knowing she might be with them, watching over them.

His grandmother continued, her voice filled with warmth. "We also light the candles to symbolize the light that guides us through our own journeys. Just as our loved ones need guidance to find their way back, we too need light to navigate life's challenges."

Pablo was beginning to understand the depth of the tradition. "So, it's like...we're helping them, and ourselves, find our way?"

Her eyes shone with pride as she continued. "Exactly, hijo. You're learning the ways of our ancestors. Day of the Dead is a celebration of love, family, and resilience. We honor those who came before us, and we find strength in their memory."

Her wrinkled face sparkled, "Later, we'll visit your mother's grave, just like we visit Abuelo's every year. We'll take flowers, her favorite food, and candles to welcome her spirit back to us."

Pablo nodded, feeling a mix of emotions: sadness, love, and a hint of excitement.

As night fell, they made their way to the cemetery, the air crisp and cool. Pablo carried a bouquet of traditional orange marigolds and a small dish of his mother's beloved pan de muerto.

His grandmother led the way, her candle casting flickering shadows on the ground. Her gray-streaked hair was pulled neatly into two braids and fastened with a bright red ribbon. She wore her clean red apron to match her traditional full-length skirt.

She carefully picked her way around other groups of people huddled around a family member's grave. Pablo looked up to see his friend Maria, shyly wave to them as Abuela greeted her family as they passed. Maria's grandmother had passed away when she was a baby.

When they reached the grave, Pablo's heart swelled. His mother's name, *Sofia*, shone in the moonlight, surrounded by vibrant flowers and colorful trinkets. His father and grandmother began to arrange the offerings, whispering prayers and stories of his mother's life.

His grandmother reverently fingered the rosary beads around her neck, her lips moving silently as she murmured the familiar Novena for the Dead. Pablo had heard these prayers before, their soothing cadence and gentle rhythm a comforting reminder of his grandmother's faith.

Pablo breathed in the cool November air, rich with the scent of flowers, earth, and copal incense. He gazed up at the star-filled sky, wondering if his mother's spirit was truly with them. How could he know if she was there? His grandmother seemed to be sure.

As they lit the candles and incense, the cemetery seemed to transform into a warm, inviting space. His hands trembled as he placed the basket of food near his mother's grave. He looked up at his father, his eyes searching for reassurance.

"Will Mamá come and eat this, Papá?" Pablo asked hesitantly. He wasn't sure what he believed, but he wanted to hold onto the hope that his mother was still with him somehow.

His father nodded, lost in thought, as memories of his beloved wife flickered through his mind.

His grandmother's face, etched with lines of love and loss, smiled softly. "Yes, Pablo," she replied. Her hands, worn from years of labor, gently covered Pablo's as they stood together before the grave.

"We bring her favorite foods, and she will be with us," she whispered. "In here," she touched Pablo's chest, "and here," she touched her own heart.

Pablo closed his eyes, took a deep breath, and imagined his mother standing beside him. He pictured her warm smile, the gentle sparkle in her eyes, and the soft touch of her hand on his shoulder. In his mind's eye, she was as vibrant and full of life as the colorful offerings before them. He imagined the scent of her cooking, the sound of her laughter, and the comforting warmth of her embrace. For a fleeting moment, the ache of her absence seemed to ease. Maybe she was with him.

The vibrant colors of the traditional dishes and fresh flowers - the fiery oranges and yellows of the marigolds, the brightly painted pottery filled with food and drink - seemed to clash with the somber atmosphere of the cemetery. The bright hues, typically associated with joy and celebration, contrasted staunchly amidst the weathered headstones, and the quiet reverence of the mourners.

Yet, as Pablo gazed upon the offerings, he began to see the beauty in this combination. The colors, though bold and lively, also represented the vibrant spirit of his mother, the love and laughter she had brought to their lives, and the memories they had shared together. In this context, the clash of colors became a striking reminder that even in death, there is still beauty, still life, and still love.

His gaze shifted to his father, cradling baby Sofia in his arms. The little one's eyes sparkled in the candlelight, and Pablo's heart swelled with love for his sister. As his father gently rocked Sofia, his eyes closed, and a soft smile spread across his face. For a moment, Pablo thought he saw a glimmer of peace, a sense of comfort, wash over his father.

It was as if he had found comfort in this moment, surrounded by the memories of his wife, Sofia, and the presence of their child who carried her name. Pablo wondered if his father felt his mother's spirit around them, watching over them.

The sight of his father, lost in thought yet seemingly at peace, filled Pablo with a mix of emotions. He felt a pang of sadness, knowing his father still missed his mother dearly, but also a sense of hope, seeing him find comfort in their family's traditions.

As Pablo watched, his father opened his eyes, and their gazes met. For a brief moment, they just looked at each other, the only sound was the soft crackling of candles and the distant chirping of crickets. Then José Pablo smiled, and Pablo returned it, feeling a sense of connection, of understanding, between them.

He whispered a soft prayer, hoping his mother could hear him, but the silence that followed left him wondering. Was she truly there? Could she feel his love as strongly as he felt hers?

Chapter Two

La Virgen

Pablo gazed out of the window of his family's small home in Guadalajara, Mexico, watching the vibrant scene come alive with the sounds and smells of his community. The scent of fresh tortillas and roasting chilies wafted through the air as his grandmother and aunts prepared for his party. Meanwhile, Pablo's thoughts, were elsewhere. His fingers instinctively reached for the gold chain around his neck, his thumb tracing the familiar contours of the small Virgin Mary pendant that hung from it. His mind wandered back to that fateful day, two days after his seventh birthday when his world had shattered into a million pieces.

He recalled the feeling of his mother's frail hand in his, her skin was cold. She beckoned him closer. With a trembling hand, she placed the pendant around his neck, her eyes looking into his with a deep sadness. "La Virgin… for your protection, my son," she whispered, her voice barely audible. "Never forget, she's always with you."

Pablo's thoughts swirled with the memory of his mother's labored breathing and the sterile smell of the hospital room. He had felt so helpless as he watched her slip away, his small body trembling with fear and confusion. The sound of his father's anguished cry still echoed in his mind.

His grandmother had placed her hands on his heaving shoulders and whispered, "She's with the saints now, Pablo. She's watching over you from heaven."

But as he grew older, doubts crept in, like shadows in the evening light. Were the stories of the saints and the Virgin Mary mere fantasies or was there truth in the legends? The pendant, once a symbol of comfort, now felt like a reminder of what he had lost.

The Virgin's gentle face seemed to stare back at him, a reminder of his mother's love. Yet, Pablo's doubts lingered, and he couldn't help but feel that there must be more to life than the rituals and traditions that had been passed down to him. Little did he know, his life was about to take a dramatic turn.

Pablo's 14th birthday was supposed to be a celebration, yet he felt uncertain about the future. He would need to start making money to help support his family.

His thoughts were interrupted as his best friend Carlos burst into the room. "Pablo, I've been looking for you everywhere!" he said, smothering him in a boyish embrace.

Pablo laughed and hugged Carlos back, his heart lifting at the sight of his friend. "What's up, hermano?"

Pablo looked up, forcing a smile. "I'm good! What's up?"

But Carlos noticed that his friend's eyes didn't quite match his smile. He sat down beside Pablo, his expression softening. "What's wrong? You seem a little down."

Pablo shrugged, trying to brush it off, but Carlos's concern was genuine. Pablo sighed deeply, "Well, I don't know… Can I tell you something?"

Carlos's face softened, and he sat down beside Pablo. "Of course, amigo. What's going on?"

Pablo took a deep breath. "I miss my mom, Carlos. I miss her so much it hurts."

Carlos nodded, his eyes filled with compassion. "Yeah, I miss her too. She was the best."

Pablo felt a lump form in his throat, which he tried to swallow. "Yeah...I just wish she was here, you know?"

Carlos put a hand on Pablo's shoulder. "I know, man. Me too."

The two friends sat in silence for a moment before Carlos spoke up. "Remember your first day of kindergarten?"

Pablo smiled, despite his tears. "How could I forget? I cried because I wanted my mom. You came over and gave me a piece of candy, and we've been best friends ever since."

Carlos grinned. "Yeah, I knew even back then that you were someone special. And I'm glad we've stuck together all these years."

Pablo felt a sense of gratitude towards his friend. "Me too, Carlos. Me too."

Carlos patted him on the shoulder again, this time more gently. "We'll get through this together, okay? And we'll support each other."

Pablo had always felt like Carlos was the older brother he never had. He was only one year older than Pablo, but he seemed more mature somehow. Mamá had always said that Carlos was born older.

They had grown inseparable, sharing countless moments together. Carlos possessed a gift of knowing exactly what to say to lift Pablo's spirits and make him feel better. He offered advice whenever Pablo found himself in a tough spot, and his words had a soothing effect on Pablo's worries and fears.

Pablo, on the other hand, had a knack for getting himself into difficult situations, and was still learning to navigate his emotions. They were the perfect pair.

Just then, Pablo's dad walked into the room. "Come on, hijo. Everyone is here!"

Pablo looked up, expecting to see his dad in his usual casual attire. But instead, he was taken aback by the sight before him.

His dad stood tall, wearing a classic white hat, and a crisp, cream-colored guayabera that seemed to glow in the soft light of the room. His boots were polished to a deep shine, and he looked...different. More put together than Pablo had seen him in a long time.

"Órale, Papá," Pablo said, surprised. "You look… really handsome."

His dad chuckled, his eyes crinkling at the corners. "Gracias, hijo. I figured I'd dress up for the party tonight. Your mom would want me to look my best."

Pablo felt a pang in his chest at the mention of his mom, but he pushed it aside and smiled. "Yeah, she would. You look great, Papá."

His dad smiled back as he playfully tipped his hat at the boys. Carlos and Pablo erupted into spontaneous laughter as they pushed at each other and followed the older man out into the night air thick with the noise of festivity.

Sofia, Pablo's little sister, twirled around, her long, dark braids bouncing with each step. She was a tiny, vibrant thing, her bright smile lighting up the space. She danced with abandon, her small hands waving in the air as she sang along to the music.

As Pablo watched, Sofia's eyes locked onto his. She held out her hands to him, beckoning him to join her. "Pablo, hermano! Dance with me!" she exclaimed, her voice full of joy.

Pablo's heart burst with love for his little sister. He had always felt a deep sense of responsibility for her, and made it his mission to ensure she felt loved, cared for, and cherished.

He couldn't help but smile as he watched her carefree dance. For a moment, he forgot about his troubles and let Sofia's infectious enthusiasm draw him into the warmth of the party.

As the music reached its climax, Sofia threw her arms around Pablo's waist, hugging him tightly. "I love you, hermano!"

she exclaimed, her voice muffled against his chest.

Pablo hugged her back, feeling a sense of peace wash over him. For a moment, everything else faded away, and all that mattered was this little ball of sunshine in his arms.

Maybe La Virgen was truly watching over him. He pushed the thought aside, eager to forget about it for now and focus on enjoying his party. Religious worries could wait; tonight was for celebration.

Chapter Three

The Party

The party was in full swing, the vibrant colors and lively music were filling the courtyard. Traditional dishes like pozole and birria were spread out on the tables. The smell of tepache wafted through the air, transporting Pablo back to his uncle's wedding day. He remembered the sun beating down on this same courtyard, the sound of the mariachi band playing "El Mariachi" as his uncle, Juan-Carlos, and his bride, Mariana, slow-danced. Pablo's grandmother had dressed him in a tiny suit and tie, making him feel like a miniature version of his uncle.

The girls from the community were dancing to the rhythm of the marimba, their bright skirts swirling around them like a kaleidoscope of colors.

Aunt Luciana's vibrant arch of balloons, adorned with bright yellow, fiery red, and sky blue hues, towered above the party. It's rainbow of colors reminded him of his party a few years ago at the game arcade.

In the corner, a lively mariachi band played with passion and energy, their music filling the courtyard. The five musicians, dressed in matching black suits with silver embroidery, performed in perfect harmony. The lead singer's powerful voice soared, accompanied by the energetic rhythm of the guitarist. Then the trumpet boldly belted out a solo, followed by the soaring melody of the violin, and the steady beat of the bass. The music filled the party with joy and excitement, drawing everyone in.

Time seemed to lose all meaning as the party wore on. Guests arrived at their own pace. Pablo's friends and family mingled and laughed, lost in the warmth of the moment. The music played on, and the dancing began, spilling out into the courtyard like a joyful tide. The night air was alive with the thrill of connection and community.

After everyone had eaten, Abuela appeared with a majestic smile, carrying a magnificent birthday cake adorned with candles, its beauty captivating the scene. The crowd erupted in cheers and applause as she placed the cake in front of Pablo.

"At last, it's time for cake!" Aunt Luciana exclaimed, her eyes twinkling with excitement. She raised her hands and began the traditional chant.

The crowd enthusiastically joined in, chanting: "Mordida! Mordida!" (Take a bite!)

Pablo's face lit up with a mix of embarrassment and delight as he leaned forward, his eyes fixed on the cake. The chanting grew louder and more insistent: "Mordida! Mordida! Mordida!"

As he lowered his face to take a big bite out of the cake, Carlos, his best friend, snuck up behind him, a mischievous glint in his eye. Just as Pablo's teeth were about to sink into the cake, Carlos playfully smashed Pablo's face down into the dessert, covering him with a thick layer of icing and colorful sprinkles. The crowd erupted in friendly laughter and cheers.

Pablo's eyes widened in surprise, and he struggled to free himself from the sweet assault. Carlos burst into laughter!

Abuela gasped in mock horror, "Carlos, shame on you!" while trying to stifle a grin.

Pablo emerged from the cake, his face a rainbow of icing and sprinkles, a sheepish grin spreading across his face. The crowd cheered and clapped, and Carlos high-fived Pablo, still chuckling.

"Happy birthday, amigo!" Carlos exclaimed as Pablo wiped the icing from his eyes. "Some things never change!" Pablo said playfully.

Pablo's gaze drifted around the courtyard, taking in the familiar scene of laughter and celebration. But his eyes landed on a figure that seemed out of place in the midst of all the joy. His father was sitting alone at a table, slowly savoring his plate of food. Pablo's heart went out to him, remembering the way things used to be.

Before his mother's passing, she was the one who brought the party to life. She was the spark that ignited the laughter, the one who coaxed his father onto the dance floor, and the one who playfully wiped icing on his nose during cake cutting. Pablo's father, on the other hand, had always been a bit more reserved, content to observe from the sidelines.

But now, without his mother's radiant presence, his father seemed lost, like a ship without an anchor. Pablo noticed the way he sat, slightly hunched, his eyes fixed on the food in front of him.

It was always Abuela and Aunt Luciana who seemed to make things happen. They were the ones who planned and prepared the family meals and organized the celebrations and gatherings. His father, on the other hand, had always been content to take a backseat, to let the women in his life handle the details.

Family meals and events hadn't ever been his thing. He would show up, of course, and smile and chat, but it was clear that he was out of his element. He was a quiet, introspective man, happier with a newspaper than with a crowd of people.

But now, without his mother to fill the void, his father's lack of involvement was more noticeable. Pablo couldn't help but wonder if his father felt lost.

Pablo's thoughts were interrupted by Sofia tugging on his arm. "Pablo, Pablo!"

Her eyes sparkled with excitement as she jumped up and down. "Where's the piñata?" she asked, her voice full of anticipation.

Pablo chuckled and shook his head. "This is a party for older kids, remember?"

Sofia's face fell, "Why?" she asked.

Aunt Luciana reached her arms out to Sofia, her dark eyes sparkling with understanding, "Sofia, sweetie, Pablo is too old for a piñata now. He's a young man."

As Aunt Luciana smiled and spoke, Pablo couldn't help but notice the familiar curve of her lips and her shiny, long black hair flowing down to her waist. She and his mother had looked so much alike.

Sofia pouted, as Aunt Luciana continued, "However, when your birthday comes around, we'll make sure to have a piñata just for you, okay? We'll fill it with candy and treats, and you can be the queen of the party." She hugged Sofia tightly, who erupted into loud laughter at the promise!

It was past midnight by the time the party had quieted down some, but Pablo's mind was still alive with the excitement of the night. He began to help his grandmother and aunts clear off the tables as he suddenly noticed that Carlos had disappeared after they cut the cake. It wasn't like his best friend to leave without saying goodbye, but Pablo shook the strange feeling off and focused on sweeping the courtyard.

He smiled contentedly at the sight of Sofia sleeping soundly on top of one of the tables and scooped her up into his arms as she let out a small sigh. He tucked her into her bed and headed for his own. He would have to wait until tomorrow to find out where Carlos had gone.

Chapter Four

Carlos's Secret

Pablo's eyes slowly opened, heavy with sleep, as the enticing aroma of Abuela's café de olla (a traditional Mexican coffee) and quesadillas wafted into his room. He stretched, still half-asleep, and let out a yawn. But as he sat up, he suddenly recalled Carlos's unexpected departure from the night before.

Pablo got out of bed and headed to the kitchen, where the delicious aromas were coming from. He slid into his chair at the table, still trying to shake off the remnants of sleep. Abuela placed a steaming cup of coffee and a quesadilla in front of him, the aroma filling the air.

"Buenos días, hijo," she said, gently patting him on the head.

Pablo mumbled a quick, "Buenos días, Abuela. Gracias!" as he hastily downed his coffee and began devouring his steaming quesadilla, his mind already focused on finding Carlos.

He had thoroughly relished his time off from school during the summer, reveling in the carefree days that stretched out before him like a blank canvas waiting to be filled with adventure. His days had been stuffed to the brim with unbridled energy and excitement, as he spent hours romping around with his playmates until the sun dipped below the horizon and the streetlights flickered to life.

They had forgotten about time while they were playing soccer in the empty lot on the corner. Pablo loved playing soccer with Carlos and his school mates, drawing a makeshift field with chalk and competing in friendly matches that lasted for hours.

He was always the first one chosen for the team, and he took pride in his skills, dodging and weaving around his opponents with ease. Carlos, on the other hand, was the master of trick shots, and their friendly rivalries kept them pushing each other to be their best.

But amidst the joy and freedom, Pablo knew that these carefree days were numbered. School would be starting soon, and with it, a new chapter in his life would begin. His father had promised Don Pedro, the owner of the local school supplies store, that he would start working for him once the new academic year kicked in.

He couldn't wait to find Carlos so they could organize a soccer match. Pablo finished his last gulp of coffee and hurriedly stood to his feet. As he turned to head out the door, he was stopped by his father's voice, "Ah, Pablo, since you're going out, I need you to take this step ladder back to Don Pedro at the edge of town. He's been asking for it."

Pablo nodded, taking the small ladder from his father, and heading out the door.

"And don't forget to say goodbye to your Abuela," his father reminded him somewhat sternly.

Pablo turned sheepishly to this grandmother and kissed her on the cheek, "Adios, Abuela. Thank you for breakfast."

Abuela smiled and patted her grandson on the cheek, "Dios te bendiga (God bless you), Pablito."

He would have to do his errand first. Soccer could wait.

Some time later, Pablo emerged from the woods, the bright sunlight a stark contrast to the dense foliage he had just left behind. He had been walking for about twenty minutes having taken a shortcut back after completing his errand. The sounds of the trees and birds began to give way to the distant hum of cars and the chatter of people.

As he walked, Pablo's mind wandered to Carlos, who had been struggling lately. He wondered where he was now.

As Pablo rounded a bend in the trail, Carlos suddenly stumbled out from behind a tree, his eyes wide with pain and fear.

"Pablo! Amigo!… Thank God I found you!" Carlos gasped, clutching at his side.

Pablo rushed to his friend's side, horror etched on his face. "Carlos, what happened? You're bleeding!"

Carlos winced, his face pale. "I got caught in the crossfire...

I don't have much time. Please, Pablo, I need a favor."

Carlos seemed to regain his strength for a moment as he tried to reassure his friend. He had blood dripping from his fingers as he pressed a worn backpack into Pablo's hands.

"Complete my run, just this once... Please, Pablo. I can't do it. It's a drop-off site, no one will see you."

Pablo hesitated, unsure of what to do. But Carlos's desperate gaze wore him down.

"Where do I need to go?" Pablo asked, feeling a sense of trepidation.

"Leave the backpack in the trashcan on Calle del Sol, near the Virgin's Shrine." Carlos instructed, his voice weak. "It's on the edge of town; no one will suspect anything. Just make sure it's done by midday."

Pablo's head reeled as he felt a sense of unease. "I'll do it, Carlos. But you have to promise me you'll get help, okay?"

Carlos smiled faintly. "I promise, amigo. Now go, please... I'm running out of time."

With a heavy heart, Pablo shouldered the backpack and set off toward the edge of town, the weight of his friend's secret pressing down on him. Why hadn't Carlos confided in him about his troubles earlier? He was entangled with dangerous people.

Pablo hastened his pace, the seriousness of the backpack's contents bearing down on him. He had to get rid of it, and fast.

He scanned his surroundings, his eyes darting back and forth until he spotted the designated street, Calle del Sol. With a sense of urgency, he dropped the backpack quickly into the trashcan and turned to leave, hoping that no one had seen him.

He broke into a cold sweat worrying about his friend, but he was also concerned that he would be tied into whatever Carlos was involved in. He knew he should be a good friend, but wondered where Carlos's loyalties lay.

He looked down at his hands and realized there was blood on them. Knowing there was a fountain nearby, he almost ran to it in his hurry to rid himself of the stains. He had to get to the hospital.

Pablo's worry grew with each step as he knew he had to find out if Carlos was all right. As Pablo made his way through the winding streets to the local hospital, his heart raced with anxiety. He burst through the doors but was immediately stopped by a security guard.

"I'm sorry, sir. You can't come in here," she said, her voice firm.

Pablo's frustration grew. "I need to find my friend: he's missing, and I think he might be here."

His heart raced with urgency. "Is Carlos Martinez Santos here?" he asked, his voice tinged with concern.

The guard led him to the receptionist, who was typing furiously on the computer monitor in front of her. After Pablo repeated his question, her expression softened with sympathy. "Yes, he is here. But I'm afraid you can't see him right now."

Pablo's anxiety spiked. "What do you mean? I need to see him! Is he okay?"

The receptionist's tone became firm. "I'm sorry, young man; since you're not a family member, you can't enter the hospital. But I can tell you that he's receiving treatment."

Pablo's frustration grew. "But I'm his friend! I need to know if he's okay!"

The receptionist stood firm. "I'm sorry. You'll have to wait outside."

Pablo's worry turned to anger, but he knew he had to calm down. He took a deep breath and nodded. As he turned to exit the building, his mind raced with worst-case scenarios. He paced back and forth outside the hospital, his heart heavy with worry. What was happening to Carlos? Was he going to be okay?

As he waited, Pablo had a sense of foreboding, a nagging worry that something was very wrong. Time seemed to pass quickly as daylight began to fade. He reluctantly accepted that he might not see his friend that day.

His eyes caught the familiar scene of La Virgin's shrine underneath a tree. The small metal box was painted white and decorated with shiny metallic streamers. He could see the familiar face of Mary looking upwards as her hands clasped together in reverence.

Pablo methodically approached the shrine and traced the sign of a cross on his forehead as he began to murmur the only prayer he knew.

"Hail Mary, full of grace, the Lord is with thee; blessed art thou among women and blessed is the fruit of thy womb, Jesus. Holy Mary, Mother of God, pray for us sinners, now and at the hour of our death. Amen."

As he finished, he added in his own words, "Mary, if you can hear me, please look after my friend Carlos." He desperately, fingered the gold chain around his neck, grasping at the hope that someone was listening to his prayer.

"Pablo!" The voice of his father reached his ears, and Pablo jerked his head up quickly.

"What are you doing here?" José Pablo asked, placing a hand on the boy's shoulder, the concern showing on his face.

"Carlos is inside, Papá. He's hurt. I've been trying to see him, but they won't let me in." The words tumbled out of Pablo's mouth like a waterfall as his eyes searched his father's face for comfort.

His father's expression turned sympathetic. "What happened to Carlos?"

Pablo hesitated, unsure of how much he should reveal. "I don't know, Papá…."

José Pablo's eyes narrowed slightly, sensing that Pablo was holding something back; but he didn't press the issue. "It's getting late, hijo. Let's go home and come back in the morning. Maybe we can see him then."

Pablo nodded, feeling a mix of relief and guilt. He fell into step behind his dad, and they walked home in silence, the only sound being the crunch of gravel beneath their feet.

After making small talk with his grandmother over dinner, Pablo lay in bed, his mind racing with thoughts of Carlos. He couldn't shake the worry that had settled into his stomach. He tossed and turned, trying to push the thoughts away.

In the back of his mind, he worried whether anyone saw him leave the bag or wash his hands in the fountain. His grandmother had always told him that

God made good things out of bad things, but he couldn't see any good in this.

As he drifted off to sleep, his mind was filled with visions of Carlos, hurt and alone in the hospital. Pablo woke up multiple times throughout the night, his heart racing and his sheets drenched in sweat.

Finally, after what felt like an eternity, Pablo fell into a fitful sleep. His mind continued to whirl with thoughts of his friend, and he slept lightly, his body tense with worry and his heart heavy with concern.

Chapter Five

Lost

Pablo's eyes snapped open, his mind racing as he remembered Carlos's desperate face, and the weight of the backpack was still fresh in his mind. He had only managed a few hours of sleep and despite his heavy eyes, swung his legs over the edge of his wooden framed bed.

He quickly threw off the covers and got dressed, while his sister, Sofia, watched him with curious eyes. "Buenos días, Pablo. Where are you going in such a hurry?" She said reproachfully. Her little hands were on her hips as she noticed that he hadn't returned her greeting.

Pablo barely acknowledged her, he muttered a quick "Buenos días" as he rushed past his grandmother, who was diligently preparing breakfast in the kitchen.

"Abuela, I'm not hungry. I have to go," Pablo said, brushing past her.

His grandmother looked confused, holding out a steaming cup of hot chocolate. "But Pablo, you need something to eat.

You can't go out on an empty stomach."

Pablo hesitated for a moment, feeling a pang of guilt, but his concern for Carlos won out. "Gracias, Abuela. I'll take this bread." He quickly grabbed a pan dulce from the basket on the table and kissed his grandmother on the cheek.

With that, he rushed out the door, leaving his confused family behind. The bright sunlight hit him like a slap in the face, and he squinted as he straddled his bike and headed off toward the hospital.

His heart was racing as he made his way through town. The vendors on the street greeted him as he passed, but he hardly even noticed them.

The steam from a tamale cart filled the air with an earthy aroma as he rounded the corner and the hospital's white and gray face came into view. The building rose above the surrounding structures like a palm tree out of a flat landscape.

He quickened his pace. He had to know how Carlos was doing.

He threw his bike under a tree and hurriedly crossed the street, his eyes scanning the crowd for familiar faces. The scene outside the hospital was one of anxious anticipation. Families and loved ones of those inside the hospital waited nervously. Some huddled together, sharing whispered conversations and comforting embraces, while others sat or stood alone, lost in their own thoughts.

He was met with a sea of faces, all waiting for a word about their loved ones. The hospital gate was lined with people, each with their own story and reason for being there, but Pablo could only think of Carlos.

He pushed past everyone in hopes of talking to the guard about when there would be news. That's when he saw them - Carlos's sister and mom, sitting in the corner next to the bars of the green gate, their faces etched with worry and fear.

Pablo's heart went out to them as he made his way over.

"Hola," he said softly, sitting down beside them. "I'm so sorry. I've been worried sick about Carlos."

Carlos's sister, Maria, turned to him, her eyes welling up with tears. "Pablo, I'm so glad you're here. We're still waiting to hear how Carlos is."

Pablo nodded, his own eyes stinging with tears. They waited in silence, the tension building as the minutes ticked by.

Finally, a nurse called out their name. Carlos's mom stood up, her hands shaking as she grasped Maria's arm. Pablo followed them to the nurse's station, his heart heavy.

"I'm so sorry," the nurse said, her voice trailing off uncertainly. "Carlos passed away last night. We did everything we could, but… we lost him."

The nurse began to talk to the ladies about arrangements for the body, but Pablo couldn't hear anything else. He felt like he had been punched in the gut.

He couldn't breathe. He couldn't think.

He looked at Carlos's mom and sister, seeing the devastation on their faces. He turned to hug them but received no comfort as their sobbing cries filled his ears.

No, he thought, shaking his head. This can't be happening. Carlos was supposed to be okay. He was supposed to get better.

His head spinning, Pablo broke away from Maria and tore down the street towards the woods. He forgot about his bike as a torrent of emotions threatened to escape him. He had to be alone. He needed to understand what had just happened.

Carlos was gone. His friend, his brother, his confidant. Gone.

Pablo ran as fast as he could, his feet pounding the cobbled streets, trying to escape the overwhelming grief that threatened to consume him. Tears streamed down his face, and he wiped them away, not wanting anyone to see him like this. He felt vulnerable, exposed, and alone.

As he reached the woods at the edge of town, he slowed down, his breath ragged, and his heart heavy. He couldn't run anymore. Pablo allowed his emotions to take over, and he sank down onto the damp foliage, surrounded by the quiet of the forest.

He buried his face in his hands and let out a sob, the sound echoing through the woods. "I am lost without you, Carlos. You were my only real friend!" Pablo exclaimed, his voice shaking with anger and grief.

He pounded the ground with his fists, feeling helpless and alone. "Why did you have to leave me," he cried out into the stillness. "Why did you have to get hurt?"

Pablo's body shook with sobs, and he felt like he was drowning in his emotions. The pain was too much to bear. He turned to heaven and raised a clenched fist. "I asked you to help me, and you didn't hear me." He yelled upwards into an empty, quiet space.

As he cried, the woods seemed to close in around him. He was lost in his grief, and he didn't know how to find his way out. Mary couldn't save his friend, and now he was convinced that everything he had believed was a lie.

He quickly unfastened the gold chain from around his neck and stuffed it into his pocket. The chain seemed to mean less now as his mother's beloved Mary hadn't come through for him in his moment of desperation.

His grief turned to anger, hardening his heart into despondency.

The next few hours were a blur as Abuela prepared tamales to take to Carlos's parents and ironed everyone's dark-colored outfits. As night fell, the family stepped into the night and prepared to silently trace the familiar path toward his friend's house.

There were several neighbors already heading toward the main street, the white candles flickering in the dark.

Abuela lit the candles that they all carried and they began the torturous walk.

Pablo was in shock. He could no longer cry. He didn't want to see his friend in a casket. He didn't know if he could handle the weight of this grief. He glanced at his father, who seemed unmoved and somber. He was carrying a pot of tamales and seemed focused on the task at hand.

Pablo wondered if people's hearts grew harder as they aged and if one day he would be as stern and unemotional as his father seemed.

Pablo glanced up to see the satin black bow displayed over the doorway to Carlos's courtyard. He knew all too well what that bow meant. His father had explained it to him in hushed tones when his grandmother had hung one just like it over their door a few years before.

This ominous bow could be seen over doorways throughout the town. It would be left there until it was discolored by the sun and battered to pieces by the wind. The bow meant that someone in this house had died. He detested that ugly bow because it meant that Carlos was really gone.

He walked into the living room, followed by his Abuela, Sofia, and his father. The warm glow of candles and the soft murmur of hushed conversations surrounded them. The air was thick with the scent of incense and the sweet aroma of café de ollá wafted from the cups held by the mourners.

Pablo quickly left his candle on the floor next to the others. There was an empty space awaiting the casket in the middle of the living room. His grandmother set down a basket of white flowers and let out a quiet sob.

Abuela's eyes scanned the room to find Ana Maria, Carlos's mother, who sat in a chair, her body shaking with sobs. Abuela rushed to her side, embracing her tightly.

"Mi hija, I'm so sorry," she whispered, holding Ana Maria as she wept.

"¿Por qué, Dios mío? Why did you take my baby boy?" she wailed, her voice cracking with anguish.

Pablo's own heart seethed with the same desperate question, the weight of his grief mirroring hers. He clenched his fists in frustration, his back pressed against the wall as he retreated into the corner. His cheeks felt hot and he cast his eyes downward in a mixture of anger and despair.

Just then, the hushed conversations abruptly stopped as the body was delivered to the house. The family members' whispers turned to wails as they cried out Carlos's name, reaching out to touch the casket as it was brought in.

The funeral attendants solemnly positioned the coffin, their faces a mask of somber respect. They wore black suit pants and matching white shirts. With a gentle nod, they lifted the lid, revealing Carlos's pale, serene face, frozen in eternal repose.

The sobs grew louder, and his mother laid over the casket, kissing the piece of glass that covered Carlos's face over and over. The glass was slightly fogged but it couldn't hide the gray hue in Carlos's complexion.

Maria gently arranged the candles at the foot of the coffin, her hands moving with reverence. Pablo watched, frozen in place, as the soft glow of the flames danced across Carlos's lifeless face. He remembered the stories Abuela used to tell him, about how the candles helped guide the spirit into the afterlife. The light was creating a path for the spirit to follow.

Pablo's mind was a loud jumble of conflicting thoughts and emotions. He wasn't sure what he believed anymore. The familiar rituals and traditions that had brought him comfort in the past now felt empty and hollow.

As Maria stepped back to admire her handiwork, Pablo felt a pang of guilt for not being able to muster the same devotion. He wanted to believe that the candles would guide Carlos's spirit to a peaceful place, but his heart felt cold and disconnected.

Pablo felt anchored to his spot, it was as though he was in a nightmare, unable to respond or move. He felt like a statue as he observed the scene. He was trapped in a sea of uncertainty. The candles, once a symbol of hope and comfort, now seemed like a distant reminder of a faith he was struggling to hold onto.

Sofia's hand tightened around his, but he didn't respond. He didn't want to approach the coffin, but he knew he had to say something to Carlos.

The room was filled with the loud cries of the mourners, the sound echoing off the walls. Ana Maria's wails were the loudest, her raw grief was unrelenting. Abuela held her close, whispering words of comfort, but even she couldn't hold back her own tears.

As Pablo approached the coffin, his heart was racing with emotion, he felt an overwhelming urge to speak to his friend. He opened his mouth to say something, anything, to Carlos's still form, but instead, the confession that had been holding him captive tumbled out.

"Carlos, I'm so sorry," he whispered, his voice cracking with grief. "I should have stayed with you instead of taking that backpack... This is my fault."

The words hung in the air, daring Pablo to confront the truth. He felt a wave of shame and regret wash over him. Pablo's eyes settled onto Carlos's face, searching for forgiveness, but there was only silence. The stillness of his friend's body was a stark reminder of what was lost.

Pablo's tears fell freely now, as he whispered again, "I'm so sorry, Carlos. I'm so sorry. I love you so much, amigo."

Chapter Six

Empty Confessions

Pablo sat at his desk, staring blankly at the test in front of him. He was 17 now, but the pain of losing Carlos still felt like a fresh wound. It was a black hole in his heart, sucking up all of his motivation and purpose.

He tried to focus on the questions, but his mind kept wandering back to his friend. He remembered the way Carlos used to make him laugh, the way he always had his back. Pablo's eyes began to sting as he fought back tears. He had failed his grade and was attempting to test out so he wouldn't fall further behind. His father wasn't happy that that he had been unable to bring in any steady money to help with the household expenses.

Suddenly, he couldn't take it anymore. He abruptly stood up and walked out of the classroom, leaving his test unfinished. The proctor called after him, but Pablo hastened his steps and didn't look back.

Pablo walked out of the school, feeling lost and aimless. He didn't know what he was doing or where he was going. He just knew he couldn't stay.

As he hurried down the street, he stumbled upon a small arcade he used to visit with Carlos. Without thinking, he pushed open the door and stepped inside. The familiar sounds of video games and laughter surrounded him, but it only made him feel more empty. He wandered over to their favorite game, a classic racing simulator, and started playing.

He lost himself in the virtual world, trying to outrun his thoughts and emotions. As the night wore on, Pablo's memories grew fuzzy, but the pain in his heart remained. He thought about his mother and felt a pang of guilt. This wasn't the kind of man he wanted to be. He didn't know how to face his family or himself.

Eventually, the arcade closed, and Pablo found himself back on the streets, feeling just as lost and alone. He slowly made his way home, wondering if he'd ever find a way to escape the pain.

Pablo walked down the streets of his hometown, his feet carrying him on autopilot as his mind wandered. Everyone he passed seemed distant, their smiles and greetings barely registering. He felt like a ghost drifting through his own life.

As he turned a corner, the familiar spire of the Catholic Church came into view. It looked like a solemn grey statue rising above the colorful houses and buildings that lined the streets. Pablo's heart stirred, seeking solace in the familiar. He pushed open the heavy wooden doors and stepped inside.

He was immediately greeted by a huge portrait of the Virgen Mary, looking down on him from above the doorway. His fingers automatically traced the sign of a cross on his forehead and back down to his heart. He lifted the gold chain on his neck and kissed it as he gazed reverently into Mary's lifeless face. He paused for a moment, trying to feel something, but nothing changed.

The scent of incense and old wood drew him in, transporting him back to a time when life was simpler. He gazed up at the stained glass windows, their vibrant colors filtering the sunlight. The gold trimmed walls were lined with life-sized statues of the saints, Jesus, and Mary. The pictures and relics were displayed on shelves that jutted out from the frames in the walls.

Suddenly, he was a child again, standing in this very church, dressed in a starched white suit, clutching his First Communion candle.

He remembered the pride in his parents' eyes as he recited his memorized prayers, and the way his mother had beamed as he received the host for the first time. He recalled the taste of the wafer, and the sweetness of the juice. It was a day of innocence, of pure joy.

But as the memory faded, Pablo's gaze fell upon the altar, and his heart sank. That was a lifetime ago.

Pablo approached the benches and took a seat. His hands gripped the wood in front of him and he dropped to his knees on the red kneeling bench on the floor between the benches.

He tried to pray, but the words stuck in his throat.

As he sat there, a sense of desperation crept in. Was this all there was? Was this lonely, hollow feeling all he had to look forward to?

Pablo's eyes wandered, searching for something, anything, to cling to. But like the people on the street, the church seemed distant, unreachably far away. The words of his grandmother rang in his ears: "God is always just a confession away." He headed towards the confessionals as a last resort.

Pablo knelt in the confessional booth, his heart racing with desperation. He hadn't been to confession in years, but he had nowhere else to turn. He took a deep breath and began to recite his list of wrongdoings, each word tumbling out on top of the one before.

"I'm failing in school. My friend died because of me. I abandoned him when he needed me. I've lied to my parents, Father. I can't keep a job. I am a terrible person." Pablo's heart overflowed with sadness as he sobbed.

The priest listened indifferently, his voice a monotone hum. "Go on, my son."

Pablo continued, unloading his guilt like a burden that he couldn't let go of. "I've abandoned my friends, my family. I've lost myself, Father. I don't know who I am anymore." His sobs were no longer quiet as Pablo finished.

The priest's tone remained unchanged, his face was hidden from view by the lattice booth. Pablo reached out to touch the wooden frame, seeking some comfort in the quietness.

"You are very far from God. You need to do a pilgrimage, my son," the reply was cold and emphatic. "If God is going to listen to you again, you must show your devotion." The silence that followed felt like an anchor that weighed Pablo's soul to the darkness.

Pablo felt shattered. A pilgrimage? Was that really the answer? He knew it wouldn't free his heart; it wouldn't erase the scars of his pain.

"But, Father, I've done so much wrong," Pablo said, his voice cracking. "I don't know if I can be forgiven."

The priest's tone hardened. "Forgiveness is not for me to give, my son. But if you want to be heard, you need to show your commitment. Do the pilgrimage, and maybe, just maybe, God will listen."

Pablo slumped forward, defeated. The priest's words felt lifeless, he felt that nothing could erase the emptiness inside him. He left the confessional booth feeling more lost than ever.

Pablo emerged from the church, the gray sky mirroring his mood. Raindrops began to fall, drumming a somber beat on the pavement. He hardly noticed, his heart too heavy to feel the gentle touch of the rain.

As he walked, the droplets soaked through his shirt, chilling his skin. But Pablo didn't flinch, his senses numbed by his pain. He felt like he was drowning in his own despair, the rain merely a reflection of the storm raging inside him.

He trudged through the streets, his feet carrying him home. The rain intensified and puddles formed on the sidewalk, Pablo walked right through, the water seeping into his shoes. He felt nothing.

His mind replayed the priest's words, "Maybe…. maybe, God will listen." Pablo knew it was a hollow promise, a desperate attempt to cling to hope. He felt like he was already lost, forever trapped in this abyss of his own making.

The rain-soaked streets blurred together as Pablo walked, his eyes fixed on some point ahead. He didn't see the people passing by, didn't hear their umbrellas snapping open. He was alone in his misery, the rain his only companion.

Pablo walked into the house, the warm glow of the living room enveloping him like a hug. His grandmother, rose from her armchair, her eyes lighting up with love. She opened her arms, and Pablo fell into them, letting her envelop him in a warm embrace.

"Ah, hijo, how are you?" she asked, clutching his face in her soft hands. Her eyes searched his, noting the emptiness in his gaze.

Pablo tried to muster a smile, but it faltered. "I'm just tired, Abuela," he said, his voice barely above a whisper.

Abuela's expression softened with sympathy. She stroked his hair, her touch soothing. "Come, sit down, eat something. You look like you haven't eaten in days."

Pablo followed her to the kitchen. The aroma of rice and mole filled the air, as his grandmother heated the food. But even the familiarity of home couldn't fill the throbbing emptiness in his heart.

As they sat down to eat, his grandmother reached out and took his hand. "We named you after Saint Pablo, you know," she reminded him, looking at him fondly. "He was a great apostle, a man of faith and conviction."

Pablo looked away, feeling a pang of guilt. He didn't feel like a man of faith, not now. He felt lost and empty.

Abuela squeezed his hand. "You're a good boy, Pablo. You'll find your way again. You need to go with me to mass tomorrow."

Pablo forced a smile, trying to reassure her. But deep down, he wondered if he'd ever find his way back to the light. He knew for certain that the confessional hadn't made his heart feel lighter. How could he find peace and freedom from his wrongdoing?

Chapter Seven

The Stranger

Pablo woke up early that next morning before the sun had fully risen. He lay in bed for a moment, thinking about the day ahead. He had decided to take action, to find work and start rebuilding his life. He would work until he had enough money for the pilgrimage. He had to try.

Without making a sound, Pablo slipped out of bed and got dressed in the dark. He didn't want to wake his grandmother or the rest of his family. They would only try to ask him questions that he didn't want to answer.

He slipped out into the cool morning air, taking a deep breath as he walked away from the house.

He walked to the center of town where the local vendors were already selling steaming tamales wrapped in corn husks. As he waited in line, he noticed a stranger standing off to the side. The man was American, with a kind face and piercing blue eyes. He seemed out of place.

The air was filled with the scent of the sweet, creamy breakfast drink called "atole". The woman in front of him ladled some of the thick drink into a Styrofoam cup and handed it to a worker in front of Pablo.

The strange man walked over candidly. "Mind if I join you?" he asked, his strong American accent unmistakable.

Pablo shrugged, and the man stood beside him, undeterred by Pablo's disinterest.

"My name's John," he said, holding out his hand. His face erupted into a smile as Pablo lifted his hand.

Pablo felt a sense of curiosity. What did this man want with him?

"Would you like to grab a cup of coffee with me?" John asked as the wrinkled woman handed them their change. "I have an important message for you."

Pablo hesitated, unsure if he should trust this stranger. But something about John's warm smile put him at ease. He was curious what the gringo may have to say to him.

"Okay," Pablo said, following John to a nearby café.

As they sipped their coffee, John leaned in, his eyes were kind as he said, "Do you know that God loves you?"

Pablo was taken aback by the question. No one had ever told him that before. In fact, he had always felt like he was on his own, that the people who had truly cared had abandoned him.

"What do you mean?" Pablo asked, his curiosity piqued.

"I mean that God loves you, no matter what you've done or where you've been," John explained. "He wants a relationship with you, and He's willing to forgive you for anything."

Pablo snorted. "I've done some pretty bad things," he said. "I don't think God would want anything to do with me."

"That's not true," John said gently. "God loves you, and He wants to help you. He wants to give you a new life!"

Pablo felt a spark of hope ignite within him. Could this be true? Could God really love him, no matter what?

"Tell me more," Pablo said, leaning forward.

The man smiled and took out a leather-bound book from his bag. "Let me read something to you out of the Bible," he said, opening the book to a page marked with a ribbon.

"John 3:16 says, 'For God so loved the world, that he gave his only begotten Son, that whosoever believeth in him should not perish, but have everlasting life.'"

Pablo listened, mesmerized, as John read the familiar words. He had heard them before, but never like this. Never with such conviction and love.

"What does it mean?" Pablo asked, feeling a sense of wonder.

"It means that God loves you so much that He sent His only Son to die for you," John answered. "He wants to give you eternal life, a life with Him. All you have to do is trust in Him."

Pablo felt tears prick at the corners of his eyes as he blinked in disbelief.

John turned to another page in his Bible. "John 14:6 says, 'Jesus saith unto him, I am the way, the truth, and the life: no man cometh unto the Father, but by me.'"

Pablo looked at him questioningly as John continued.

"This verse means that Jesus is the only way to heaven," John explained. "He's the only way to have a relationship with God. You can't get to God through good works or religion. You can only get to Him through Jesus."

Pablo felt a sense of clarity wash over him. He had been trying to find his way to God through his own efforts, but it hadn't worked. Maybe this was the answer. Maybe Jesus was the way. Was this why he didn't feel relieved after confessing his sins to the priest?

"But what about the Virgin Mary?" Pablo asked, confused. "I've always been taught to pray to her, to ask for her intercession. Does she take people to heaven?"

John smiled gently. "The Bible doesn't teach that," he replied. "While Mary was a special person, chosen by God to be the mother of Jesus, she's not the way to heaven. Jesus is the only way. We can't rely on anyone else to get us to God, not even Mary."

Pablo was starting to understand. He had been taught to rely on Mary and the saints to intercede for him, but now he was starting to see that Jesus was the only one who could truly help him. He felt as though a light was being turned on in his soul.

John leaned in, his eyes locked on Pablo's. "Listen, Pablo, I know you're hurting. I know you're searching for answers. But I want you to know that there's a bigger picture here. See, sin separates us from God's great love. It's like a chasm, a gap that we can't bridge on our own."

Pablo frowned, unsure of where John was going with this.

"But here's the thing," John continued, "God loves us so much that He sent His only Son, Jesus Christ, to die on the cross for us. That sacrifice, Pablo, that's what bridges the gap between God and man. It's the only thing that can. The Bible tells us that Jesus is the mediator between God and man. In 1 Timothy 2:5, it says, 'For there is one God, and one mediator between God and men, the man Christ Jesus.'"

John's eyes sparkled with enthusiasm as he continued, "And it's not just about Jesus bridging the gap, Pablo. It's about how we receive that gift. Ephesians 2:8-9 says, 'For by grace are ye saved through faith; and that not of yourselves: it is the gift of God: Not of works, lest any man should boast.'"

Pablo frowned, thinking back to his conversation with the priest. "But Father Michael told me that I need to do a pilgrimage to be forgiven of my sins. He said it's the only way to make amends."

John's expression turned gentle. "Pablo, that's not what the Bible says. It says that our salvation is a gift, not something we can earn through works. Jesus already paid the price for our sins on the cross. We just need to accept that gift, to trust in Him."

Pablo looked confused, torn between the priest's convincing words and John's heartfelt message. Deep within, he felt a glimmer of hope, a sense that maybe, just maybe, he didn't have to carry the weight of his guilt anymore.

Pablo shook his head, feeling a mix of confusion and skepticism. "I don't understand," he said.

John smiled gently. "It's not about understanding, Pablo. It's about faith. It's about trusting that God's love is bigger than our sins, bigger than our pain. And it's about accepting that love, that sacrifice, for ourselves. Salvation from sin is a gift. The work has already been completed on the cross."

John leaned closer, reading Pablo's face carefully. "Is God speaking to you right now, Pablo? Would you like to accept God's forgiveness today, Pablo? Would you like to place your faith in Jesus Christ right now?"

Pablo looked away, feeling a lump form in his throat. No one had ever spoken to him like this before. No one had ever told him the truth so emphatically about God and what He wanted. He knew that this was what he needed.

"Yes," Pablo said finally, his voice filled with conviction. "I want to trust in Christ. I want to accept His gift of salvation."

John's face broke into a wide smile. "Praise God, Pablo!" he exclaimed. He put his hand on Pablo's shoulder, and his eyes closed in prayer.

"Dear Heavenly Father," John prayed, "I thank You for Pablo's decision to trust in You. Thank you for dying on the cross to pay for his sins and mine. Help his understanding and guide him on his journey with You. In Jesus name I pray, Amen."

As John finished praying, Pablo felt a sense of peace wash over him. He looked upward, toward heaven, and spontaneously prayed as well.

"Thank You, God," Pablo said, his voice filled with emotion. "Thank You for loving me, for forgiving me. I don't deserve it, but I accept Your gift of salvation. Please help me to follow You, and to live for You."

Tears streamed down Pablo's face as he prayed, and he felt a weight lift off his shoulders. He knew that his life would never be the same again.

John smiled and squeezed Pablo's shoulder. "Welcome to the family of God, Pablo," he said. "You are now a child of God, and He will never leave you or forsake you."

Pablo grinned, feeling a sense of joy and peace that he had never known before. He knew that God had sent this stranger to speak to him today.

"Hey, Pablo," John said, standing up to leave. "Would you like to meet again tomorrow at the same time? We can grab coffee, and I can tell you more about God's plan for your life."

Pablo nodded enthusiastically. "I'd love to," he said. "I need to learn more."

John smiled. "Great! I'll meet you here at 12 pm tomorrow. We'll dive deeper into the Bible and explore what it means to follow Jesus."

Pablo nodded, already looking forward to their next meeting. He watched as John walked away, feeling a sense of gratitude and wonder at the unexpected turn his life had taken.

As he sat there, sipping his coffee, Pablo couldn't help but feel a sense of hope and excitement for the future. He knew that he still had a lot to learn, but he was eager to see where this was going.

Chapter Eight

A Second Chance

As Pablo slowly opened his eyes, a warm light flooded his soul, illuminating the dark recesses of his heart. He felt a sense of weightlessness as if the crushing burden of his past mistakes and pain had been lifted, replaced by an unshakeable hope. The air seemed fresher, the world brighter, and his spirit renewed.

He lay in bed for a moment, savoring the peace that settled over him like a gentle rain. The memories of his past still lingered, but they no longer held the power to define him. He felt reborn, remade, and rejuvenated like a once withered plant now blooming with vibrant color.

Pablo's thoughts turned to the events of the previous day, and he smiled, recalling the moment he had surrendered his life to Christ. The tears he had shed, the prayers he had whispered, and the sense of forgiveness that had washed over him – it all seemed like a dream, yet more real than anything he had ever experienced.

With a sense of wonder, Pablo swung his legs over the side of the bed and planted his feet firmly on the ground. He felt a sense of purpose, a sense of direction, and a sense of belonging he had never known before. He knew that he still had a long journey ahead, but for the first time in his life, he felt equipped to face whatever challenges came his way.

As he stood up and began to get ready for the day, Pablo caught a glimpse of himself in the mirror. He barely recognized the person staring back – the same eyes, the same face, but a completely different soul. He smiled, feeling a sense of joy and gratitude that he had never thought possible. He knew that he had been given a second chance at life, and he was determined to make the most of it. Today was the first step towards his new life.

As he walked out of the bedroom, Sofia looked up from her breakfast at the table, "Buenos días, hermano!" She called cheerfully, thrusting her arms up for a hug.

Pablo ran over and playfully planted a kiss on her cheek, "Buenos días, Sofia."

Sofia's eyes couldn't hide her surprise as she noticed how happy her brother seemed. It had been a while since she'd seen him light up like this, his usual struggles momentarily forgotten in a rare burst of joy. The happiness radiating from his face was a welcome sight.

Pablo ran over to the sink where his grandmother was washing dishes and hugged her tightly, wrapping his arms around her shoulders. He was already much taller than his grandmother, a sturdy woman whose once strong, broad shoulders had grown more frail with age.

"I love you, Abuela. Thank you for always taking care of us, Pablo said with renewed gratitude and love.

His grandmother wiped her arms on her blue-laced apron and wrapped them around Pablo's neck. "I love you, hijo!" She said simply, her wrinkled face beaming with love.

"What's going on, Pablo?" Sofia asked, unable to hold back her curiosity any longer.

Pablo plopped down on the chair beside her and looked into her skeptical eyes lovingly. "Sofia, I found God yesterday…"

He excitedly began to explain everything about meeting John and learning about salvation. He was grateful that she had given him a chance to explain what had happened in his heart, and he knew that he needed to learn more. He suddenly felt that God wanted him to tell everyone that he knew about this newfound joy.

As time went on, Pablo lost interest in the things that used to consume him: pressure to fit in, missing his mother, worrying about school and grades, and even what had happened to Carlos. He no longer found pleasure in the things that had once brought him temporary happiness. He felt satisfied. He found joy in his relationship with God, in reading the Bible, and in sharing his faith with others.

Pablo spent more time with John after school, and his life continued to transform. He learned about God's love and forgiveness, and the sacrifice Jesus made on the cross. He realized that God wanted to use his life to help others.

After a few weeks, Pablo learned that he needed to get baptized. He excitedly assented, wanting to take this 'first step in obedience', as John called it.

Finally, the day arrived. Pablo had invited his sister to join him in this special moment. Sofia was unsure what this meant for Pablo, but she couldn't contain her excitement as she had watched Pablo's whole outlook change. She had to see for herself what this was all about.

Pablo stood at the edge of the lake, his heart racing with excitement and a hint of nervousness. The whole congregation was there. Everyone was beaming with the excitement of the moment. He recognized a few people from town standing on the bank, offering encouragement to their new brother in Christ.

John, a gentle smile on his face, placed a hand on Pablo's shoulder.

"Pablo, my brother, you have come to this moment of obedience following Christ's example. Are you ready?"

Pablo blinked in the sunlight, knowing that this was an important step "Yes, I am ready."

"Then let us begin," John said calmly as he led Pablo into the still waters of the lake.

John raised his hand, a smile rested over his lips. He closed his eyes and began to pray, "Dear Heavenly Father, we come before You today to witness the baptism of Your child, Pablo. Thank you for saving him and changing his life! Amen!"

"Buried with Christ in baptism… " John's gruff voice trailed off as Pablo closed his eyes, feeling the cool water envelop him. John's hands guided him downward.

"… raised to new life in Him!"
As Pablo emerged from the water, he felt a rush of joy and peace flood through him. He opened his eyes to see John smiling at him, and the warm sunshine on his face. He heard voices of support and

encouragement as the congregation clapped softly.

John gripped Pablo's hand and pulled him in for a warm hug, "I am proud of you, Pablo. Remember, God is always with you."

Chapter Nine

Purpose

Pablo knew God wanted to use him to share his faith with his family. "God, give me strength." Pablo prayed silently as he headed home one night after prayer service at church.

The sermon had challenged him that he may be his family's only chance to hear the Gospel. He recalled John's words, "We are the light of the world. It is our lives that bring others to Jesus."

He knew that his mother had never heard the true Gospel. God had given him the opportunity to know the truth about Jesus and why His death mattered. He had to share this with his family. The Gospel was too good to keep to himself!

Pablo took a deep breath as he stepped into the house, his heart racing with anticipation. He knew this conversation wouldn't be easy, but he was prepared. He and John had spent hours going over the verses and he already knew what their questions would be.

"Papá, can we talk?" Pablo asked, his voice cracked slightly. He pulled out a chair and joined his family at the dinner table.

His dad looked up from his plate, worry lines creased his brow. "Of course, Pablo. What's going on?"

Pablo hesitated, his eyes scanning the dinner table. Sofia was chatting with Abuela, oblivious to the tension. He took another deep breath and began.

"Papá, I need to tell you something. I've found God. I've been going to a Christian church lately, and God has given me peace. I know that this new faith is the truth. I have found hope!"

His dad's expression turned stern, but Pablo pressed on feeling that the Holy Spirit was working.

"I now know more of what the Bible says. I was lost without God, but I have found forgiveness and salvation, Papá." As he finished the sentence, Pablo's eyes filled with tears and his voice quivered with emotion. "This is what I needed!" He added.

Jose Pablo's face softened, and he reached out, placing a hand on Pablo's shoulder.

"You have been sad and lonely since you lost Carlos, hijo. I am happy you are learning more about God." José Pablo's response seemed somewhat out of character and Sofia stopped talking to listen in on the conversation.

Abuela slowly got up from the table and ladled some steaming hot chocolate into a brown clay mug. She handed the cup to Pablo with a smile.

"Here you go, hijo." She said warmly.

"Gracias, Abuela," Pablo said flashing a smile at his grandmother.

He took a sip of the rich chocolate, laced with cinnamon, and reached for his Bible.

He looked around the table, his heart full of love for his family.

"You know, I've been learning about God's love and forgiveness," Pablo commented, his voice filled with excitement. "And I want to share it with you all. It's changed my life, and I know it can change yours too."

Sofia looked up, curiosity sparkling in her eyes. "Tell us, Pablo."

His grandmother smiled, her face radiant with love. His father nodded, his expression open and receptive.

Pablo opened with the question John had asked him a few weeks ago at the café. "Do you know that God loves you? Really loves you and cares about you in spite of what you have done?"

Sofia leaned toward her brother and said, "I don't know if anyone actually knows that, Pablo. One day, if we are good enough, we may reach heaven. We need to confess our sins, and attend mass, and be really good…" Her voice trailed off- and it appeared as if the more she talked, the less sure she was of herself.

José Pablo shook his head. "No one can know," he said, as he put his palms outward and scrunched his face.

"Let me read you a verse from the Bible," Pablo replied confidently as he read John 3:16 aloud to his family.

"For God so loved the world, that he gave his only begotten Son, that whosoever believeth in him should not perish, but have everlasting life."

Abuela uncrossed her arms and looked closer at Pablo's Bible as she said, "Explain that to us, hijo. What does it mean?"

Pablo beamed with love as the same Gospel message he had recently received flowed clearly from his mouth. He watched his family begin to understand the depth of who God was, just as he had.

As they finished dinner, Pablo shared his story, telling them about the Gospel and the transformative power of God's love. The room was filled with humility and tears, but most of all, hope.

He knew that the Holy Spirit was working in his family's hearts as he pressed into their doubts with verses from the Bible. As the night wore on, the doubts began to wash away in the truth that was being shared. At the end of the night Sofia bowed her head and received Jesus Christ as her Savior.

She looked upwards as she prayed a simple, heart-felt prayer.

"God, I know I am a sinner. I want You to save me. Thank you for taking my place on the cross. Amen."

She looked towards Pablo beaming with excitement. Abuela patted her lovingly on the back as Sofia wiped away a tear from the corner of her eye.

Pablo lifted his eyes upwards as his heart lifted a silent prayer of his own. "Thank you, Father. Please save my Papá and Abuela too."

Pablo could tell that his father and grandmother didn't fully understand what had just happened, but he knew. José Pablo respected the special moment, but he was strangely silent. He seemed to be thinking about the truths that his son had just confidently shared with him.

Pablo felt that God was working in the hearts of his loved ones, and he couldn't be happier. In that moment, Pablo knew he'd found his true purpose – to share the love and forgiveness he'd received with those around him. God had given him a reason to live.

Chapter Ten

Double Blessings

Pablo stood in front of the mirror, adjusting his tie and smoothing out his shirt. Many years had passed since that night at his family's table. He was getting ready for church, and he couldn't help but feel a sense of excitement and gratitude. As he looked at his reflection, he thought about how far he had come.

He thought about his friends and family, and how God was changing their lives too.

His dad, who had once been so worried about him, now beamed with pride. His sister, Sofia, had started attending church with him and was growing in her faith. His grandmother had recently been baptized.

Pablo felt overwhelmed with gratitude. He was so thankful to God for saving him, for rescuing him from the darkness, and for bringing him into the light. He thought about all the times he had tried to change on his own but had failed. But God had done what Pablo couldn't do - He had changed him from the inside out.

As he finished getting ready, he took a deep breath and let the gratefulness wash over him. He felt like he was going to burst with joy. He thought about the worship service ahead, and how he would get to sing and praise God with his brothers and sisters in Christ.

As he sat on the bed to put to pull on his dress socks, he saw the scar on the ankle that he had gotten one day riding bikes with Carlos. They had been so close for so many years, and he felt like God had saved him from the same bad influences that Carlos had gotten tangled in with.

The thought of Carlos brought mixed emotions. He knew that Carlos hadn't understood the Gospel, but he was so grateful that Carlos's parents and sister had recently accepted Christ.

"Thank You, God," he whispered, his voice trembling with emotion. "Thank You for saving me, for changing me, for using me to change others. I am so grateful to be Your child."

Pablo took one last look in the mirror and smiled. He knew that he still had flaws, that he still had struggles. But he also knew that he was not alone. God was with him, and that made all the difference.

Pablo's gaze drifted and his heart skipped a beat as he saw his wife, Rosa, standing behind him, her eyes shining with love and adoration. He felt a surge of thankfulness wash over him, grateful for the blessings God had poured into his life.

He didn't deserve a wonderful Christian woman like Rosa, but God had given him everything he needed, and more.

Pablo turned to his wife, and she smiled, her arms opening wide to envelop him. They embraced, holding each other tightly, the warmth of their love and gratitude palpable.

"Te amo (I love you)," Pablo whispered, his voice filled with emotion.

"Te amo, sweetheart," Rosa replied, her voice was clear and full of assurance.

Hand in hand, they headed to church, ready to worship and give thanks for the blessings in their lives. As they walked Pablo felt a sense of peace, knowing God had brought them together, and would continue to guide them on their journey.

After the service, Sofia turned to Pablo with tears in her eyes. "Thank you for sharing this with me, Pablo," she said. "I feel like I've been given a wonderful gift."

The two siblings embraced in the sunlight warmed by the love of God in their hearts. "Come, eat with us, sis," Pablo said warmly. "I want to tell you something."

Pablo's home was filled with the savory aromas of Rosa's cooking as he welcomed his father, his grandmother, and Sofia into their home.

Pablo was settling into the couch, sipping a glass of water. The warm glow of the midday sun streamed through the windows, casting a cozy ambiance over the room. As he chatted with his father and Sofia, his gaze drifted to the kitchen, where his wife Rosa was preparing lunch. Abuela was busily making fresh tortillas in the kitchen.

As he looked at Rosa, memories flooded his mind. He remembered meeting her in Bible college, where they had bonded over their shared faith and passion for serving others. He recalled the way she had captivated him with her intelligence, kindness, and beauty. Their late-night conversations, studying Scripture and exploring their dreams, had sparked a deep connection that had grown into a lifelong commitment.

Pablo's heart swelled with appreciation as he gazed at the woman who had become his partner, his best friend, and his soulmate. He smiled, feeling grateful for this life they had started to build together.

Just then, Rosa approached the couch, a gentle smile on her face. "Lunch is ready," she said, her voice soft and inviting.

Sofia, noticing the tender moment, smiled knowingly and nudged him playfully. "Let's eat! I'm starving!"

Abuela chimed in, "The food is getting cold, hijo!"

The family gathered around the dining table, ready to enjoy the meal and each other's company. They sat down to a delicious meal of enchiladas, rice, and beans, and Pablo raised his eyes and thanked God for their many blessings.

As they ate, Pablo and Sofia shared stories of God's faithfulness, rejoicing over the ways He had worked in their lives.

Pablo's heart swelled with excitement as he thought about the new chapter ahead.

Just seeing his grandmother sitting with a contented smile across her face reminded him of the day she had received Christ. She had grappled with questions and had really given Pablo the runaround, asking him all kinds of things while Pablo scrambled to find the Bible verses to explain the truths of the Gospel to her. It was a moment of pure joy and spiritual victory as she had finally rested her arms on the table and said, "I believe. The Bible says it, and that is enough for me."

"Familia, I have some news to share with you," Pablo said, his voice filled with enthusiasm. "God has given me an opportunity to pastor a small church on the other side of town. John has had several people come to Christ in that area, and they need a full-time pastor. I know God has prepared Rosa and I for this moment."

Sofia's eyes widened in surprise, and then a huge smile spread across her face. "¡Eso es increíble, hermano! (That's amazing, brother!)"

José Pablo clapped his son on the back, and his grandmother beamed with encouragement. "We are so proud of you, Pablito. God is with you."

Pablo clasped Rosa's hand tightly, feeling a sense of peace and confirmation. "I know it's a big step, but I feel God's leading. I'm excited to see where He takes us."

Rosa's eyes sparkled with delight as she joined in, her voice overflowing with enthusiasm. "We're both thrilled! We know God has amazing plans for us. We visited the area with John last week, and we are burdened to know that there isn't a Bible-preaching church there. There are young families and children who need to hear the Gospel."

She paused, her gaze darting briefly to Pablo before sharing their second secret,

"Also… God has blessed us with a baby!" Her words spilled out like a happy torrent, as Pablo's face broke out into a broad smile.

The room exploded into a chorus of cheers and gasps, with Sofia leaping from her chair to fold Rosa in a warm, tearful hug. This was the icing on the cake, the best news piled upon the best!

As they lingered over coffee, basking in the glow of their shared joy, Pablo felt his heart swell with gratitude for his family's unwavering support. With God's guidance and their love, he felt empowered to embrace this new chapter, ready to take the leap of faith with confidence in God.

Chapter Eleven

Pastor Pablo

Rosa's hands moved deftly as she ironed Pablo's dress shirt, her face radiant with pride. She hummed a soft tune, lost in thought, as she smoothed out the wrinkles.

Today was the day that John and several other pastors would ordain Pablo into the Gospel ministry. This day had been planned for months and everyone was excited for the big day.

Pablo sat on the edge of the bed, his eyes catching the glimmer of the gold chain he used to wear around his neck. It was a memory of his mother that he kept next to his bed. He knew that his Mom hadn't heard the Gospel before she died, and his heart ached with the burden that thousands more in his town hadn't either.

"God, please use my life to share the Gospel with others." He prayed quietly as he clutched the chain close to his heart.

He knew God had called him for this very reason into the ministry. God had brought him so far, from the depths of darkness to the threshold of being ordained into the ministry. Pablo's heart swelled with emotion as he reflected on his journey, the struggles he had overcome, and the triumphs he had experienced.

His mind went to the ordination ceremony ahead. He knew that it was a milestone, a recognition by the church that he was called to serve God's people. But more than that, it was a reminder that he was not alone in this journey - he was part of a larger community of believers who were committed to following Jesus and spreading His love to the world.

He glanced up at Rosa, who was still ironing, oblivious to his gaze. He felt a surge of love and appreciation for her, for her unwavering support and encouragement.

"Pablo, are you ready?" Rosa asked, hanging up the shirt and turning to him with a smile.

Pablo nodded, standing up, his eyes never leaving hers. "I'm ready," he said, his voice filled with conviction. "I'm ready to serve, to follow God's call, and to see where He takes me next."

Rosa's smile broadened, and she walked over to him, her pregnant belly poking out of her shirt. She rested her hands on his shoulders and looked kindly into his eyes. "You're going to be an amazing pastor,

Pablo. God has prepared you for this moment."

Pablo's heart swelled with pride as he walked into the church, Rosa by his side. The warm glow of the sanctuary received them, filled with the gentle hum of conversations and the sweet scent of flowers.

As they made their way down the aisle, Pablo's eyes met those of John, the man that God had used several years before to lead him to Christ. John's face beamed with a proud smile, and he extended a warm handshake.

"Pablo, my brother, I'm so proud of you," John said, as he drew Pablo in for a firm hug.

As Pablo scanned the crowd, his eyes landed on his family, beaming with pride, his father's warm smile and his grandmother's face radiant with joy. And in the front row, Sofia glowed with anticipation, her brown eyes gleamed like chestnuts, soft and radiant.

Pablo felt a deep sense of gratitude and love as he took in the sight of his loved ones mingled in with his family in Christ. His thoughts drifted to all the times he had served in this church, from leading small groups to preaching on Sundays. He remembered the late-night prayers, the early-morning Bible studies, and the countless hours of ministry that had shaped him into the man he was today.

He felt blessed to have had the opportunity to serve alongside such a loving and supportive community. Pablo felt a profound sense of completeness, a deep assurance of being exactly where he was meant to be.

As everyone took their seats, John's warm voice filled the sanctuary, "Welcome, everyone, to this special day."

The congregation's murmurs subsided, and all eyes turned to the front, eager to participate in the momentous service.

John continued, "We gather today to celebrate a significant milestone in Pablo's journey, his ordination into the ministry. It is a privilege to have his family, friends, and community here to support him on this special occasion. Let us come together to acknowledge God's calling on Pablo's life and commission him for the work ahead."

As the ceremony reached its most significant part, John and the two other pastors laid their hands on Pablo's shoulders. They surrounded him, their voices rising in a chorus of prayer, asking God to anoint and equip him for the ministry ahead.

As the pastors prayed, Pablo's mind wandered back to a pivotal moment—his graduation from Bible seminary in this very church. The firm handshake and diploma from John brought a sense of accomplishment that settled deeply into his heart. The memory was vivid: Abuela's tears of joy streaming down her weathered cheeks, and his father's proud smile lighting up the room.

But now, standing in the present moment, a different kind of emotion surged within him. His heart overflowed with a profound sense of gratitude and humility. He knew he was unworthy of the honor bestowed upon him, yet God had chosen him. And in this sacred moment, he surrendered completely to the divine will, ready to embrace whatever lay ahead.

Tears flowed freely down the pastor's faces, their voices thick with emotion as they prayed. Pablo's own tears joined theirs, a testament to the overwhelming joy and reverence he felt.

When the prayers concluded, the pastors surrounded Pablo in a tight embrace, their arms heavy with the weight of their blessings and support. In that embrace, Pablo felt the depth of their love, their belief in him, and the strength of their encouragement. He knew, without a doubt, that he was not alone in this new chapter of his life.

John's voice broke through the emotional haze, trembling with sincerity, "I'm so proud of you, Pablo."

Pablo lifted his gaze, pointing upward as he fought back his tears. "God deserves all the glory for saving me and turning my life around. I'm forever grateful that He sent you to share the Gospel with me and my family." The two men embraced tightly, a bond forged in faith and shared purpose.

Pablo smiled, feeling a sense of peace and purpose. God had orchestrated every step, sending John to share the Gospel at the very moment that Pablo needed it most. Through God's grace, he had reached his own family with the same message of love and hope. And now, he felt the unmistakable call to go out into his community, to be a beacon of God's truth to others.

Gripping his Bible with renewed conviction, Pablo felt a surge of pride—not in himself, but in the God who had taken him from darkness to light. He was living up to his namesake at last. Just as Paul had been a great missionary in Biblical times, Pablo knew he was being called to walk a similar path. He would to be used by God to bring others to Christ. He was ready, and with God's strength, he would fulfill his calling.

About the Author

Rebekah Anderson is a passionate writer, wife, and mother of five, dedicated to sharing the Gospel through storytelling. Raised in a Christ-centered home by her parents, she was deeply influenced by her father's commitment to his calling as a pastor and missionary. Growing up surrounded by the godly example of many missionaries shaped her understanding of eternity and the importance of ministry.

Now, as a mother and missionary herself, Rebekah continues to live in light of eternity. Four of her five children were born on the mission field and she hopes to impart the same rich heritage to them as they grow. She joyfully serves alongside her husband, Jonathan, and is active in children's and ladies ministries. Through her stories, Rebekah hopes to offer readers a glimpse into the lives of people in countries without Christ, sharing the transformative power of the Gospel.

Recommended Materials:

Embark on a 20-day devotional journey to understand and embrace your identity in Christ. Each day features a reflection, meditation, and prayer focused on who you are in Christ. Alongside your spiritual growth, explore the 20 largest cities in Latin America. Learn about their culture and history. This book offers a unique blend of spiritual discovery and cultural exploration. Join us to deepen your faith and broaden your understanding of the world.

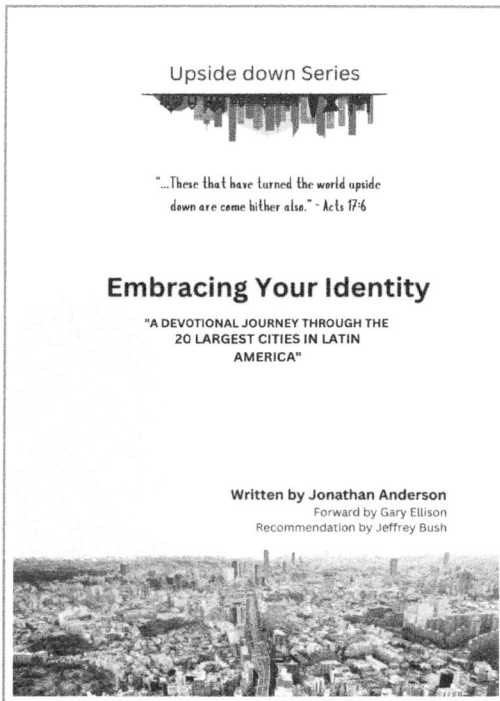

Upside down Series

"...These that have turned the world upside down are come hither also." ~ Acts 17:6

Embracing Your Identity

"A DEVOTIONAL JOURNEY THROUGH THE 20 LARGEST CITIES IN LATIN AMERICA"

Written by Jonathan Anderson
Forward by Gary Ellison
Recommendation by Jeffrey Bush

Printed in Dunstable, United Kingdom